"I'm sorry, Puss," said the miller's son. "I don't know what to do. How can I look after you without any money?"

"Don't worry," said the cat. "Just give me some boots and a bag and we'll be fine." Puss pulled on the boots, filled the bag with lettuce and marched off to a meadow.

Before long, a little rabbit hopped over to the bag and began to nibble at the lettuce. In a flash, Puss scooped up the bag and hurried off to the King's palace.

Upon meeting the King, Puss swept off his hat and bowed low. "Your Majesty," he said, "may I present you with this very fine rabbit, a gift from my master, the Marquis of Carrabas?"

The King smiled, "You deserve a treat from the palace kitchens."

While in the kitchens, Puss overheard the servants talking. The next day, the King and his daughter would be taking a drive by the river.

Puss returned to his master. "In the morning," he told him, "go for a swim in the river. If anyone asks, say that your name is the Marquis of Carrabas."

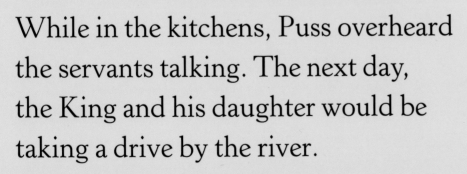

The miller's son did as Puss said. He went to the river, took off his ragged clothes and jumped in. Puss hid the clothes in the bushes.

A minute later, the royal carriage drove past, with the King and his daughter, the Princess, inside. "Stop the carriage!" cried the King. "Why, it is the clever cat who came to see me yesterday."

Puss sighed, "I wish, your Majesty, I could present my master to you today, but while he was swimming in the river, a thief stole all his clothes!"

At once, the King asked for a suit of fine clothes to be brought from the palace. The miller's son got dressed and shyly came forward.

"My dear Marquis," beamed the King, "may I present my daughter, the Princess? Do come and ride with us."

Puss scampered on ahead. He saw a man gathering hay
in a meadow. "The King will be here in a moment,"
Puss told him. "My master, the Marquis of Carrabas,
would be very grateful if you could tell the King that he
owns all the land around here."

"I can do that," said the man, "but let's hope the ogre who
lives in that castle doesn't hear me. The land is his."

Puss then hurried to the castle. When a huge ogre opened the door, Puss spoke up boldly. "I have heard," he said, "that you are a great magician. Is that true?"

"Come in," replied the ogre, "and I will show you!"

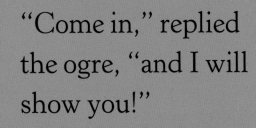

In a flash, the ogre turned himself into a fierce lion.

"Well," said Puss, "I'm sure it's easy for a big, strong ogre to become a big, strong lion. But could you turn yourself into a tiny, weak mouse?"

"Just watch me!" roared the ogre.

Puss pounced!